CHI 1/08 FRIENDS
OF ACPL

If You Prefer, I'll Use a Thermometer!

Kelly Doudna

Consulting Editors, Diane Craig, M.A./Reading Specialist
and Susan Kosel, M.A. Education

Published by ABDO Publishing Company, 4940 Viking Drive, Edina, Minnesota 55435.

Credits
Edited by: Pam Price
Curriculum Coordinator: Nancy Tuminelly
Cover and Interior Design and Production: Mighty Media
Photo Credits: Kelly Doudna, Image Ideas, Photodisc, ShutterStock, Wewerka Photography

Library of Congress Cataloging-in-Publication Data

Doudna, Kelly, 1963-
  If you prefer, I'll use a thermometer! / Kelly Doudna.
   p. cm. -- (Science made simple)
  ISBN 10 1-59928-594-0 (hardcover)
  ISBN 10 1-59928-595-9 (paperback)

  ISBN 13 978-1-59928-594-8 (hardcover)
  ISBN 13 978-1-59928-595-5 (paperback)
  1. Thermometers--Juvenile literature. 2. Temperature--Juvenile literature. I. Title. II. Series: Science made simple (ABDO Publishing Company)

  QC271.4.D68 2007
  536'.51--dc22

                                                              2006015230

SandCastle Level: Transitional

SandCastle™ books are created by a professional team of educators, reading specialists, and content developers around five essential components—phonemic awareness, phonics, vocabulary, text comprehension, and fluency—to assist young readers as they develop reading skills and strategies and increase their general knowledge. All books are written, reviewed, and leveled for guided reading, early reading intervention, and Accelerated Reader® programs for use in shared, guided, and independent reading and writing activities to support a balanced approach to literacy instruction. The SandCastle™ series has four levels that correspond to early literacy development. The levels help teachers and parents select appropriate books for young readers.

Emerging Readers	Beginning Readers	Transitional Readers	Fluent Readers
(no flags)	(1 flag)	(2 flags)	(3 flags)

These levels are meant only as a guide. All levels are subject to change.

A **thermometer** is a tool used to measure temperature. Temperature is a measure of how hot or cold something is. In science, a **Celsius** thermometer is usually used to measure temperature. In everyday life, both Celsius thermometers and **Fahrenheit** thermometers are used.

Words used to talk about thermometers:

cold	measure
cool	temperature
degrees	warm
hot	

A thermometer
shows how hot the
inside of the is.

A thermometer shows how cold the inside of the is.

Mom puts a

thermometer in

my to check

my temperature.

I stay in when my temperature is 101 degrees Fahrenheit.

The ☀ has warmed the air to 73 degrees Fahrenheit.

can fall when the temperature is 0 degrees Celsius.

If You Prefer, I'll Use a Thermometer!

Thelma thinks
her water is hot,
but she wants to be sure
whether it is or not.
She prefers to use
a thermometer
so that a good
measurement will occur.

A thermometer
is a tool
that measures how
warm or how cool.

Thelma puts the thermometer in so the measurement can begin. Thelma waits two minutes to see what the temperature will be.

At the end of that time, I look at the red line.

13

Thelma looks at where
the red line stops
and reads the number
at its top.
The water, she sees,
is 38 Celsius degrees.

The temperature
is just right
to make
hot chocolate
tonight!

We Use a Thermometer Every Day!

A meat thermometer measures how warm the roast is in the middle.

A thermometer tells you if the meat is cooked safely through.

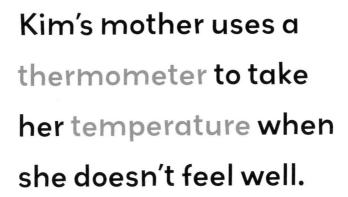

Kim's mother uses a thermometer to take her temperature when she doesn't feel well.

Kim has a fever of 101 degrees Fahrenheit.

20

Jed uses a thermometer to measure the water temperature in his aquarium.

Jed helps make sure the water stays the correct temperature for his fish.

Mike goes swimming when the thermometer outside reads 80 degrees Fahrenheit.

What other things could you use a thermometer to measure?

Glossary

Celsius – a scale used to measure temperature in the metric system.

degree – the unit used to measure temperature.

Fahrenheit – a scale used to measure temperature in the U.S. customary system.

temperature – a measure of how hot or cold something is.

thermometer – a tool used to measure temperature.